SURVIVING a Tsunami

Nicolas Brasch

Australia • Brazil • Japan • Korea • Mexico • Singapore • Spain • United Kingdom • United States

Surviving a Tsunami

Fast Forward
Blue Level 10

Text: Nicolas Brasch
Illustrations: Melissa Webb
Editor: Johanna Rohan
Design: Vonda Pestana
Series design: James Lowe
Production controller: Hanako Smith
Photo research: Gillian Cardinal
Audio recordings: Juliet Hill, Picture Start
Spoken by: Matthew King and Abbe Holmes
Reprint: Katherine Fullagar

Acknowledgements
The author and publisher would like to acknowledge permission to reproduce material from the following sources:

Photographs by AAP Image/AFP, cover, pp 1, 9, 11, 12 /EPA, p 10; Fairfax Photos/Jason South, p 15 top; Lonely Planet Images/Jerry Alexander, p 4; Newspix/AFP, p 13; Photolibrary.com/Pacific Stock, p 5 top/ Photonica, p 8/ Robert Harding Picture Library Ltd, p 15.

ISBN 978 0 17 012545 1
ISBN 978 0 17 012537 6 (set)

Cengage Learning Australia
Level 7, 80 Dorcas Street
South Melbourne, Victoria Australia 3205
Phone: 1300 790 853

Cengage Learning New Zealand
Unit 4B Rosedale Office Park
331 Rosedale Road, Albany, North Shore NZ 0632
Phone: 0800 449 725

For learning solutions, visit **cengage.com.au**

Printed in Australia by Ligare Pty Ltd
15 16 17 18 19 20 21 19 18 17 16 15

Evaluated in independent research by staff from the Department of Language, Literacy and Arts Education at the University of Melbourne.

SURVIVING a Tsunami

Nicolas Brasch

Contents

Chapter 1

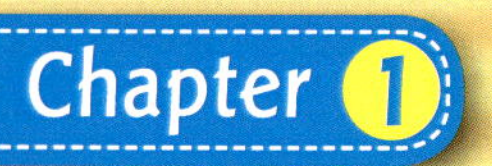

WHAT IS A TSUNAMI?

In December 2004,
I was 12 years old and lived in **Indonesia**.
I went to school and helped my family.
Life was good.

Then, on 26 December 2004, a tsunami hit many places in Indonesia.

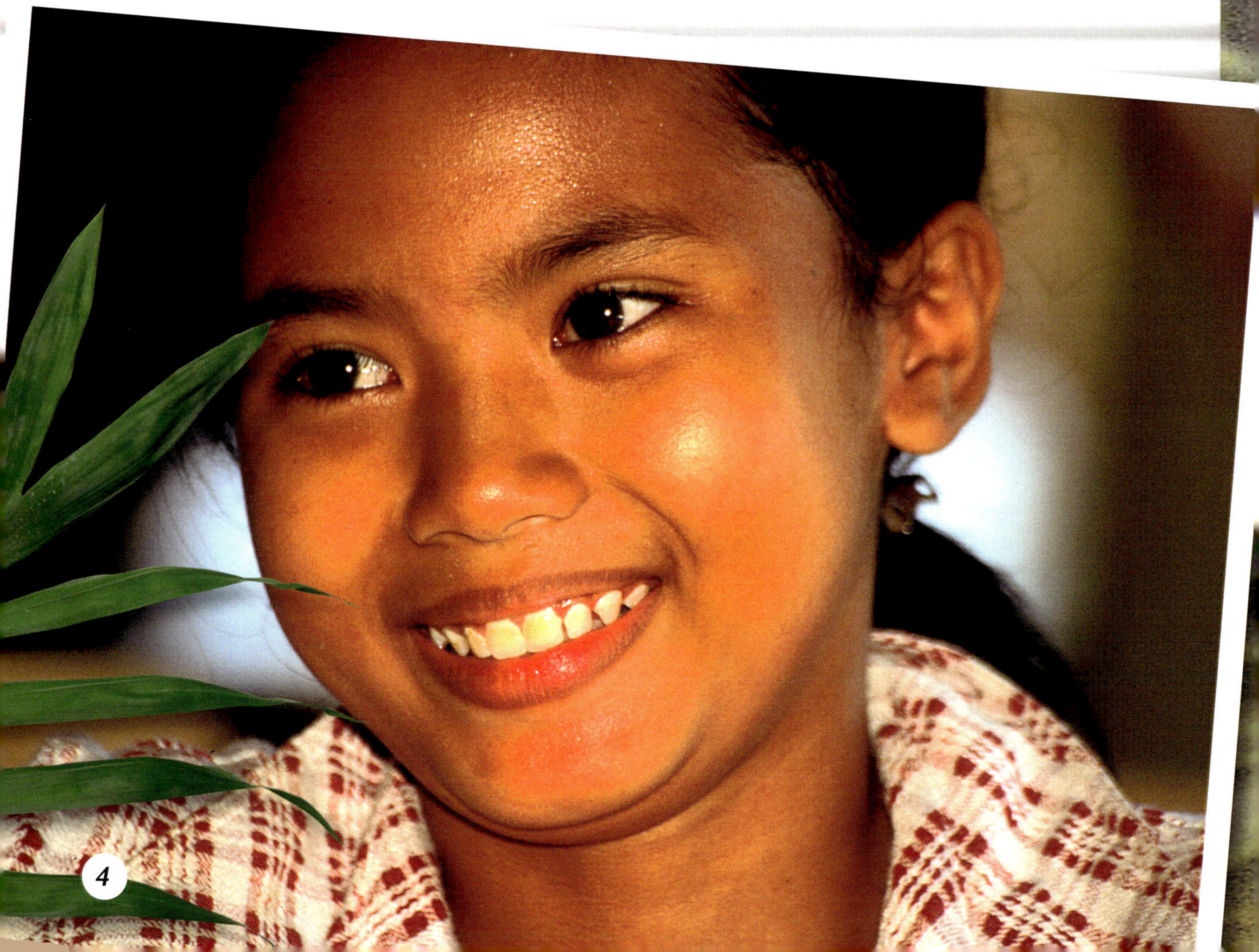

Before December 2004, I didn't know what a tsunami was.

Now I know all about them.

I even know how to say the word, tsunami.

It sounds like *soo-nar-mi*.

Some people think that a tsunami
is a giant wave, but a tsunami isn't just one wave.
A tsunami is a number of giant waves
that are set off by an **earthquake**.

The earthquake that started the tsunami in 2004 happened close to the coastline of Indonesia.

Let me tell you more...

Running Words 116

Chapter 2

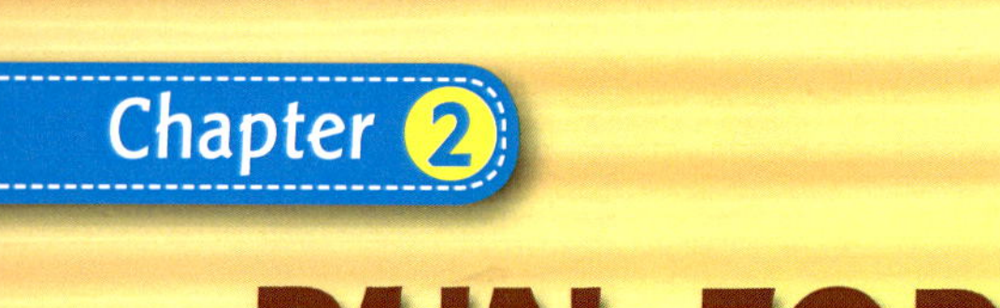

RUN FOR THE HILLS

Most days, I walked along the beach
to look for wood.
Wood is good for starting a fire.

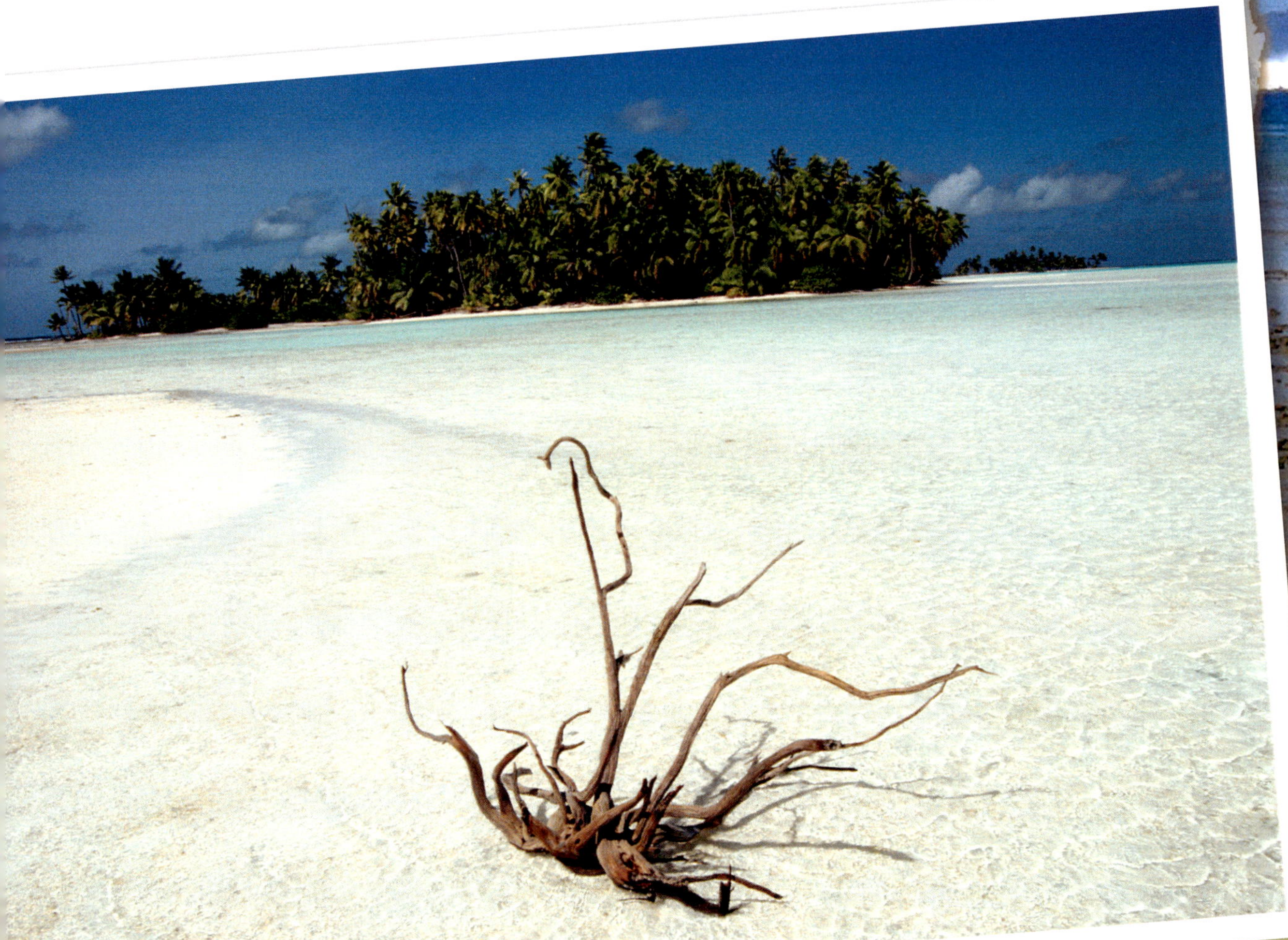

On the day the tsunami hit,
I was walking along the beach
when I saw something very odd.
The **tide** was going out
when it should have been coming in.

I raced home to tell my family.

As I ran, I heard shouting behind me.
I stopped and turned around.
People were shouting and looking at the sea.

Then, a giant wave hit the beach
and was racing over the land.
Houses and shops were washed away.

My family's house was on a hill.
I ran as fast as I could up the hill.
At last, I made it to my house
and shouted to my family
to run to the top of the hill.

Chapter 3

A DISASTER FOR THE WORLD

We made it to the top of the hill. From there, we saw the danger below.

Wave after wave crashed onto the beach
and raced over the land.
Many people couldn't run as fast as the waves
and were washed away with the houses and shops.

Later, I found out that the tsunami didn't just hit Indonesia.

The tsunami hit countries all over Asia and as far away as Africa.

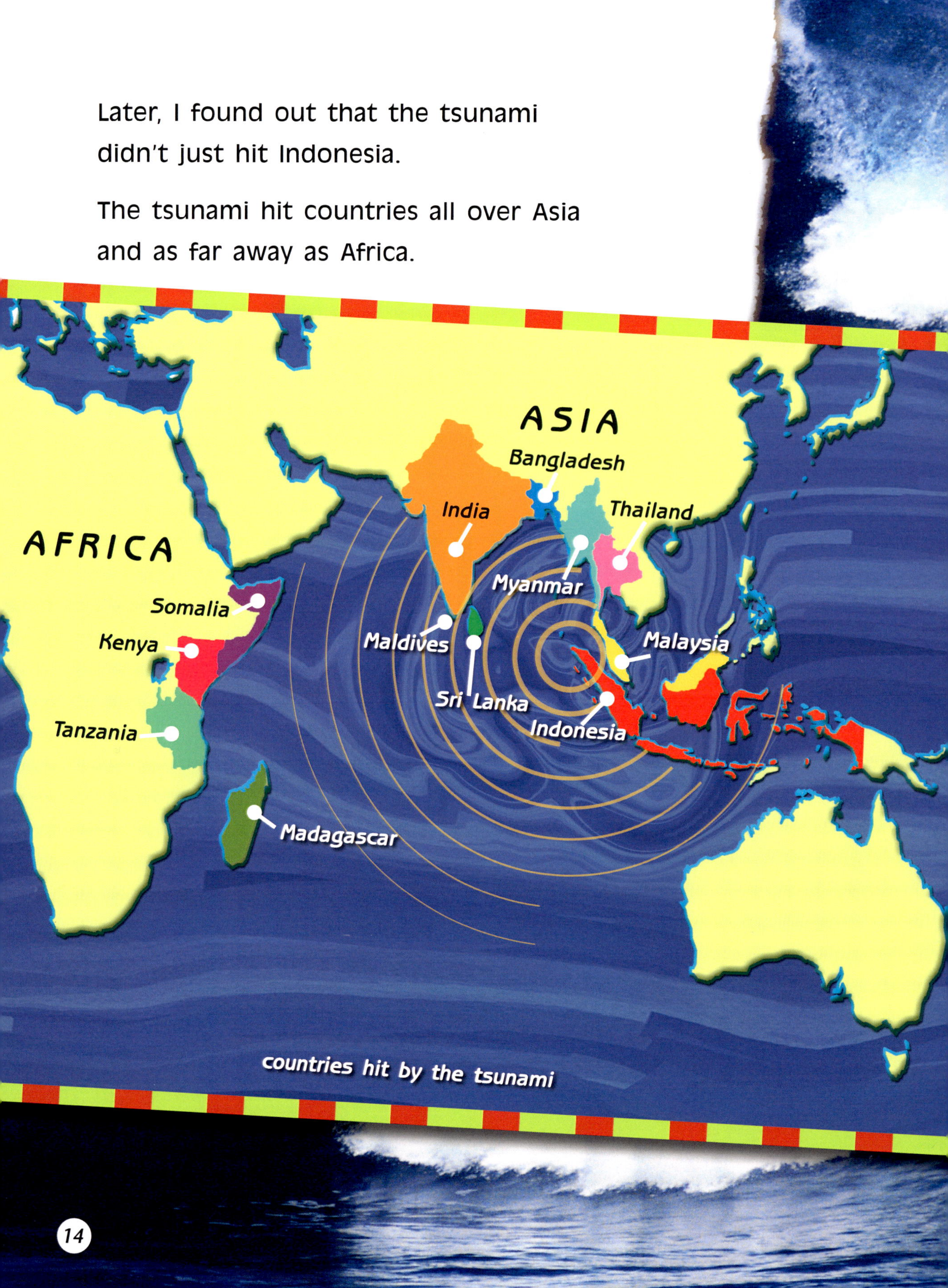

countries hit by the tsunami

I hope I never see a tsunami again.
But if I do, I will know what to do.
I will tell everyone
to run to the top of a hill.

Glossary

earthquake a violent shaking of the ground

Indonesia a country in Asia

tide the regular rising and falling of the sea

Index